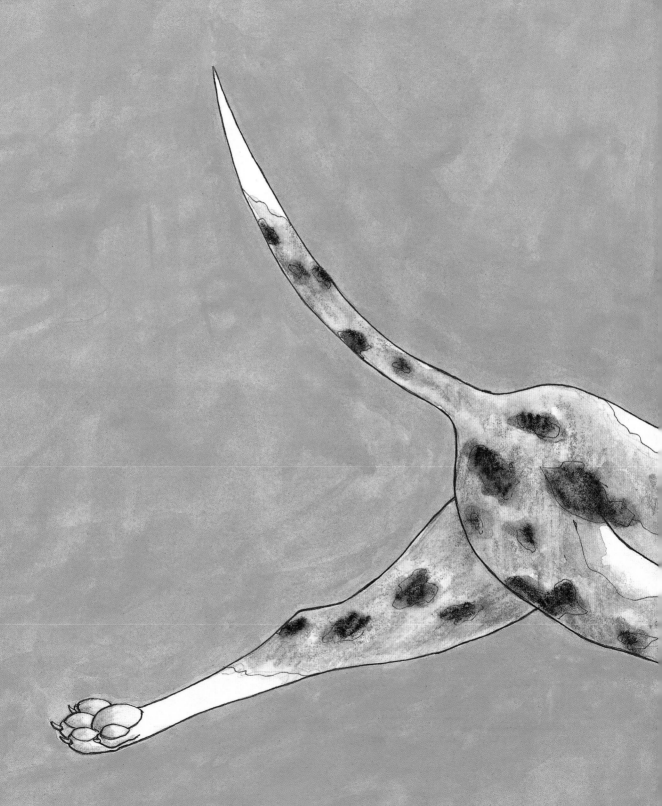

♡ + slurps —

Sudie + 🐾 Guess Who?!

Dear Calla Roo...
Love Savannah Blue

a letter to a pen pal

Mom ~
we saw this and
it made me think of
you. I especially like
the illustrations - but its not
as witty as the Pandora/Wanna
letters. Much love
lynthu

Written & Illustrated by
Sudie Rakusin

• WINGED WILLOW PRESS •
HILLSBOROUGH, NORTH CAROLINA

• Winged Willow Press •
Hillsborough, North Carolina

Published by Winged Willow Press, Hillsborough, North Carolina

For information and to order additional copies, write to:
Winged Willow Press
PO Box 92
Carrboro, NC 27510

Printed in Korea

Library of Congress Card Number: 00-104742

ISBN 0-9664805-1-1

First Edition

10 9 8 7 6 5 4 3 2 1

For Calla Ruth
K.O.T.N.

And for all those everywhere who
cherish the love that friendship brings

Dear Reader,

My name is Sudie.

I have a precious niece named Calla Ruth. She is eight years old. I live with an adorable Great Dane dog named Savannah Blue. Savannah Blue is two years old.

When Calla Ruth visited me in North Carolina, she and Savannah Blue had a wonderful time together. Unfortunately, Calla had to go back home to Baltimore. Savannah Blue was very sad. She missed her new friend so much that not even a crunchy dog bone would cheer her up.

Then I had an idea. I suggested that she and Calla Ruth become pen pals. They could write all their adventures and secrets to each other. So, even though they lived far away, they could still be friends.

This made Savannah happy and she started writing the first letter to her own pen pal that very day...

P.S. In the letter Savannah Blue calls me Soodle. I guess if I can call her Peach Pit, she can call me Soodle.

Dear Calla Roo,

I am so excited. I never wrote to anyone before. This is my first letter to you, my very own pen pal.

Since your Mom and my Soodle are sisters, does that make us sisters too, or cousins?

When I finish writing this letter, I will
wait by the mailbox for a long time
just to make sure a bird or butterfly
or squirrel doesn't take the letter
before the mail person gets here.
You can't be too careful.

This is me and my big sister,
Josie Louise. She's bigger than I am,
but I can run faster. She eats a lot.
I am a picky eater. Soodle says we
are all different and that's OK.

What are your favorite foods?
Mine are peanut butter dog bones
and grass. Yum! Oh, and also
anything that is in Josie's or Jezebel's
bowl. Do you like to eat out of your
brother Wesley's bowl?

This is my oldest sister, Jezebel. We call her Velcro Dog 'cos everything sticks to her. Things like pinecones and leaves and twigs. Jez just got a bath and a haircut. Soodle had to take this photo with her camera fast before a leaf fell on her and stuck!

I love my Bigfoot Baby you gave me. My favorite game is to run around the table a zillion times with her in my mouth until we get so dizzy we have to flop down for a nap.

The picture on the wall is me with my sisters. Josie Louise is on the left and Jezebel is in the middle. The cute blue-eyed girl on the right is guess who?

Oh, there are Stinky Pinky and Suzy Shark on the floor again.

Soodle puts out corn for the deer and sunflower seeds for the birds. She says that all animals are safe in our home.

Sometimes when we are all out in the meadow Soodle looks up, points her finger and says, "Hawk!" Then we all have to watch the hawk fly by.

I have to put sunscreen on my pink nose so it won't burn. Do you?

We all went out the other day and planted trees. Well, Soodle planted and I dug. She has to use a shovel. I just use my paws. I love to dig holes. Then I had to eat grass and throw that up! It was the best day.

↖ my buddies

I just have to be wild sometimes. You know, dig really big holes, hide when Soodle calls me, tease Jez, not listen to Josie, "Miss Leader-of-the-pack-know-it-all," until she gets so angry she wants to bite my head off. Then Soodle says, "No fighting, girls." And then I have to look like "Miss Who-me?" with my eyes as big as blue marbles.

I bet you get wild sometimes too. What bad stuff do you do?

Hey, wanna be in a wild girls' club? No goody-goodies allowed!

Josie Louise and I have two names.
Jezebel has one name. So I call her
Jezebel Stinky Smell. But Soodle
says, "We do not call our sisters
unnice names in this house." So then
I think to myself, sure, OK, whatever
you say—

Soodle Doodle looks like a stroodle
    Has arms like a noodle
    And walks like a poodle.

Oh, gosh, that was too funny, and if
Soodle ever found out I made that
up she would look at me so hard it
would make my legs shake.

bone

But mostly she loves me and calls me these love names. Here are some:

Sabana Boo	Honey Lamb
S.B.	Pumpkin
Peach Pit	Pumpky
Fur Girl	Punky Doodle
Fur Fur	Baby Girl
Bunny	Love Girl
Bun-bunny	Blue-eyed Baby Girl

What cuddle names does your Mommy call you?

Here is a photo of me, Josie and Jezebel walking in the woods. Soodle took a million of these with her camera all in one day. She kept making us stop to pose. She called them art shots. They aren't very good, but we love her anyway!

I live with all girls. We don't have a brother like you do. What's it like to have a big brother like Wes? Do you play ball together? Does he look out for you?

One day in the winter Jezebel and I went walking in the snow. We were very proud 'cos ours were the first paw prints of the whole nation in this very snow.

Do you make paw prints in the snow?

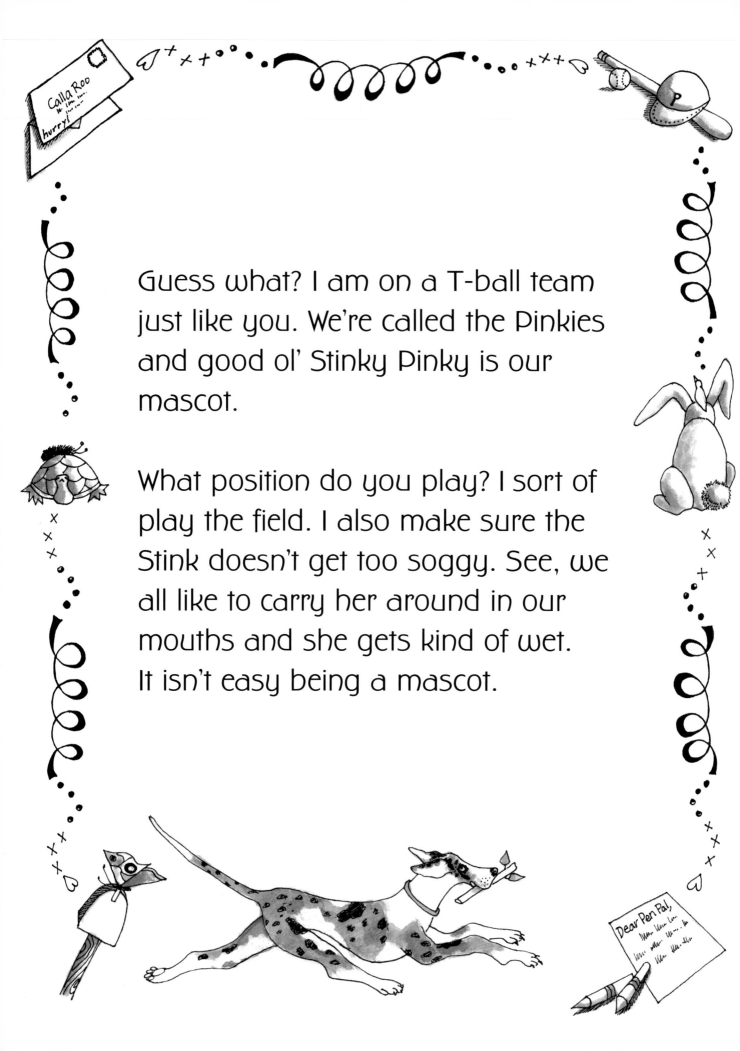

Guess what? I am on a T-ball team just like you. We're called the Pinkies and good ol' Stinky Pinky is our mascot.

What position do you play? I sort of play the field. I also make sure the Stink doesn't get too soggy. See, we all like to carry her around in our mouths and she gets kind of wet. It isn't easy being a mascot.

Here we are—me and the Stink.

We're both smiling. You might not be able to tell with me 'cos I smile without teeth.

Well, I gotta go. You know, busy day ahead—chasing butterflies, jumping over logs, sniffing the grass, playing tag, digging holes, teasing my sisters, eating treats and rolling in something really smelly.

I love you and miss you so much.

Your pen pal,

Savannah Blue

P.S. If I wait out here at the mailbox will your letter get to me sooner?

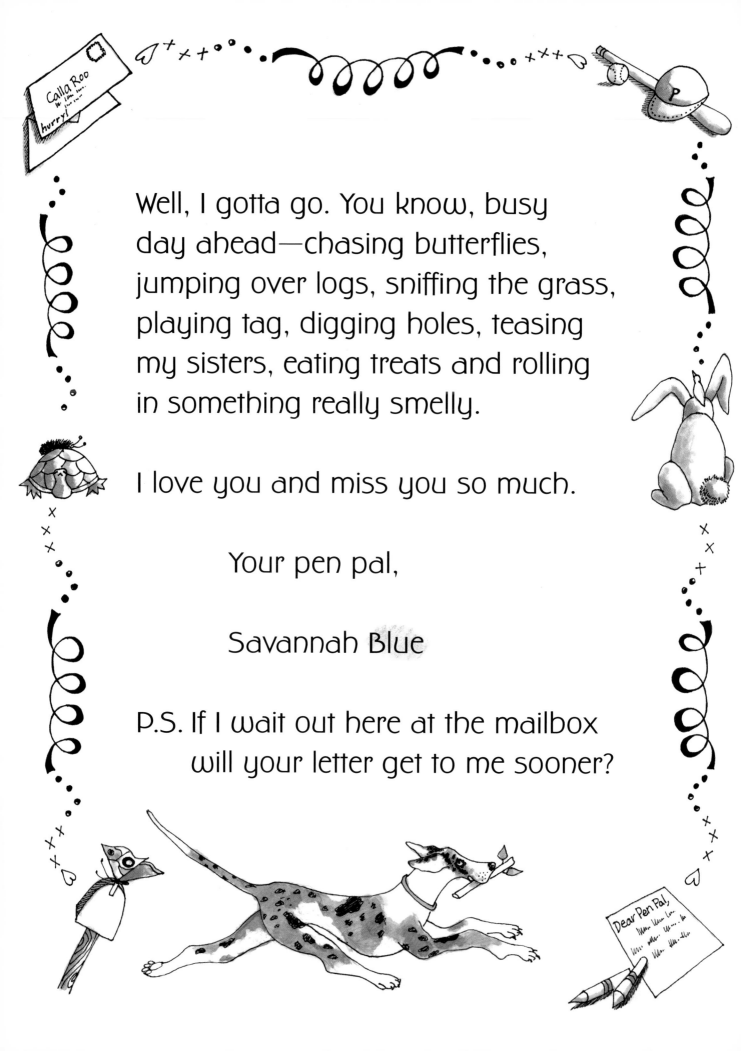

P.P.S. K.O.T.N. (kissy on the nosey)